THE
BARN

Leah H. Rogers

illustrated by Barry Root

CANDLEWICK PRESS

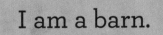

I am a barn.

I was built by many hands.
Over one hundred years ago,
ropes lifted my parts into place.
Neighbors made my structure tall and secure,
laying the foundation that roots me to the earth,
putting up the posts that hold my red cedar walls.
Triangles keep me sturdy.
Large wooden beams bear my weight.

I am a barn.

When the sun begins to grow over the treetops,
I watch as the low creeping fog lifts high into tall grass
and strands of sunlight reach through my cobwebbed windows.
My animals wait eagerly for their morning meal;
their whinnies and coos flood my aisle.

I am a barn.

My chickens amble out of my coop
to peck and dig for buried bugs.
My horses are led out of their stalls
to carry young riders on their saddled backs.

I am a barn.

My cows chomp on tall, rich grass,
shooing flies away with their swishing tails.
And the dogs romp and wrestle in my outstretched fields,
never seeming to tire of their joyous play.

I am a barn.

In the long shadows of the late afternoon,
I wait for the sun to sink,
for the air to cool.
The peepers begin their nighttime song,
and my chickens slowly wander inside.
I feel them shuffle about my coop,
fluffing up their feathers, finding their nests.
I hold the warmth that encourages the hens
to lay their eggs.

I am a barn.

A cat lurks in a distant field,
crouching to catch her unsuspecting dinner,
while I cradle her kittens in a bed of discarded blankets.
They lie wrapped together like tangled yarn,
waiting for their twilight milk.

I am a barn.

In the darkening field,
I listen as the cows amble toward my pen to rest,
while the calves run and play.
Don't they know it is time to settle down?
But the dusk air is cool,
and they are too young to care.

I am a barn.

I watch as a clever coyote
stretches in my surrounding woods.
Its long-standing trees the ideal hiding spot.
The setting sun is her wake-up call,
as darkness is the perfect time
to catch her favorite meal.

I am a barn.

Swallows softly fly
up to my deep, dark rafters,
then out the doors again.
Back and forth.
In and out.
Bringing dinner to their chicks,
who wait eagerly in mud-packed nests.
Below, the kittens are restless too,
as they still haven't had their evening milk.

I am a barn.

In the cool and clear night
my weather-worn doors are left open.
The fresh breeze of summer spreads between the stalls.
I smell it mix with the sweet scent
of freshly cut hay
and dusty horses.
I feel them restful in their stalls
lined thick with soft shavings.

I am a barn.

I see the cows have found the pen
left open for them.
The calves are tired now,
and I can feel them fold into the straw
where they will sleep side by side
and lie back-to-back.

I am a barn.

The chill night air blows quietly
down my stone aisle,
smooth from years of use.
The gentle wind cools off the dogs
that have come in to rest on my floor.

I am a barn.

All are safe within my walls.
Animals settled down deep in their bedding:
the chickens in their coop,
the horses in their stalls,
the cows in their pen,
the swallows in their nests.
Heavy, restful breathing,
warm and comforting.
I settle and wait for the morning to come
so I can watch and live the day again.

I am your barn.

For my mom
LHR

First edition 2021

Library of Congress Catalog Card Number pending
ISBN 978-1-5362-0906-8

21 22 23 24 25 26 CCP 10 9 8 7 6 5 4 3 2 1

Printed in Shenzhen, Guangdong, China

This book was typeset in Archer.
The illustrations were done in watercolor and gouache.

Candlewick Press
99 Dover Street
Somerville, Massachusetts 02144

www.candlewick.com